MW00888524

McSWEENEY'S
SAN FRANCISCO

Awake Beautiful Child

An ABC Day in the Life

Amy Krouse Rosenthal   illustrated by Gracia Lam

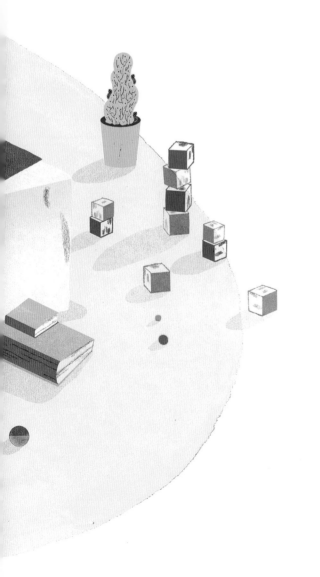

All Begins Cheerily

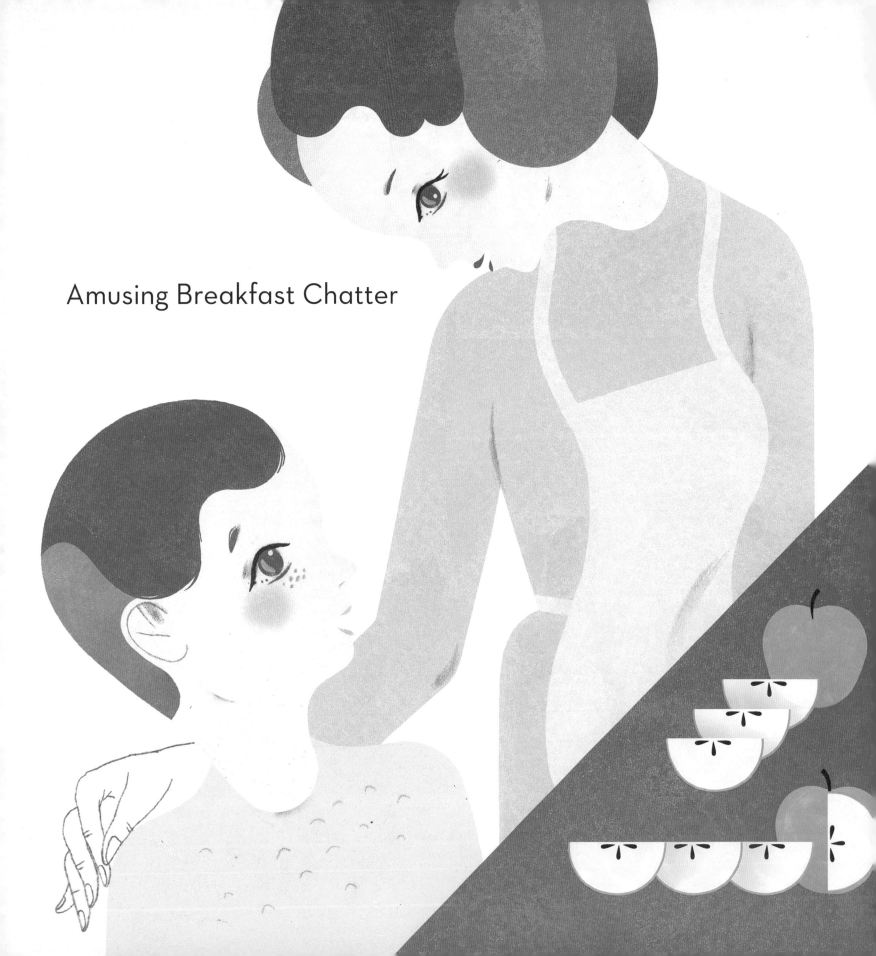

Amusing Breakfast Chatter

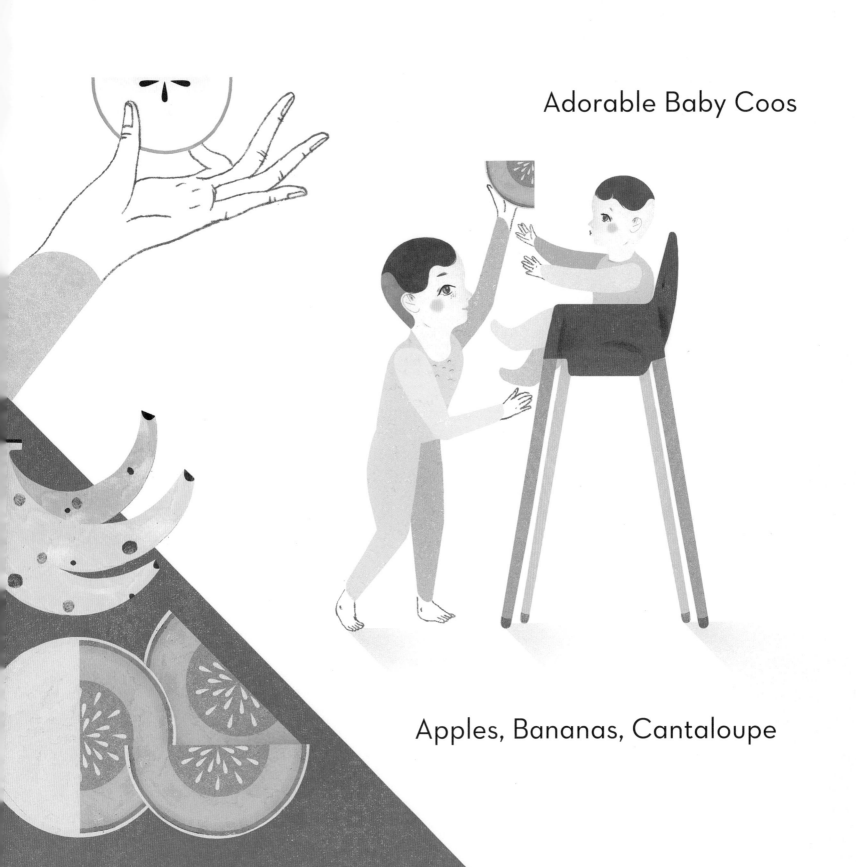

Adorable Baby Coos

Apples, Bananas, Cantaloupe

Ants, Butterflies, Caterpillars

Above, Birds Chirp

Airy Billowy Clouds

Adventurous Boy's Cape

Afraid But Courageous

"Attention! Be Careful!"

Another
Bright
Candle

Atop
Birthday
Cake

Avoid
Blinking—
Cheese!

Afternoon Brings Calm

Afar, Bells Chime

Active
Bustling
City

Around
Bouncy
Carousel

Ahead,
Bridge
Crossing

Artist's Brilliant Canvas

Assorted Bright Colors

Applause!
"Bravo!"
Curtsy!

Always Be Curious

Almost-Bedtime Countdown

Abundant Bubbles Clean

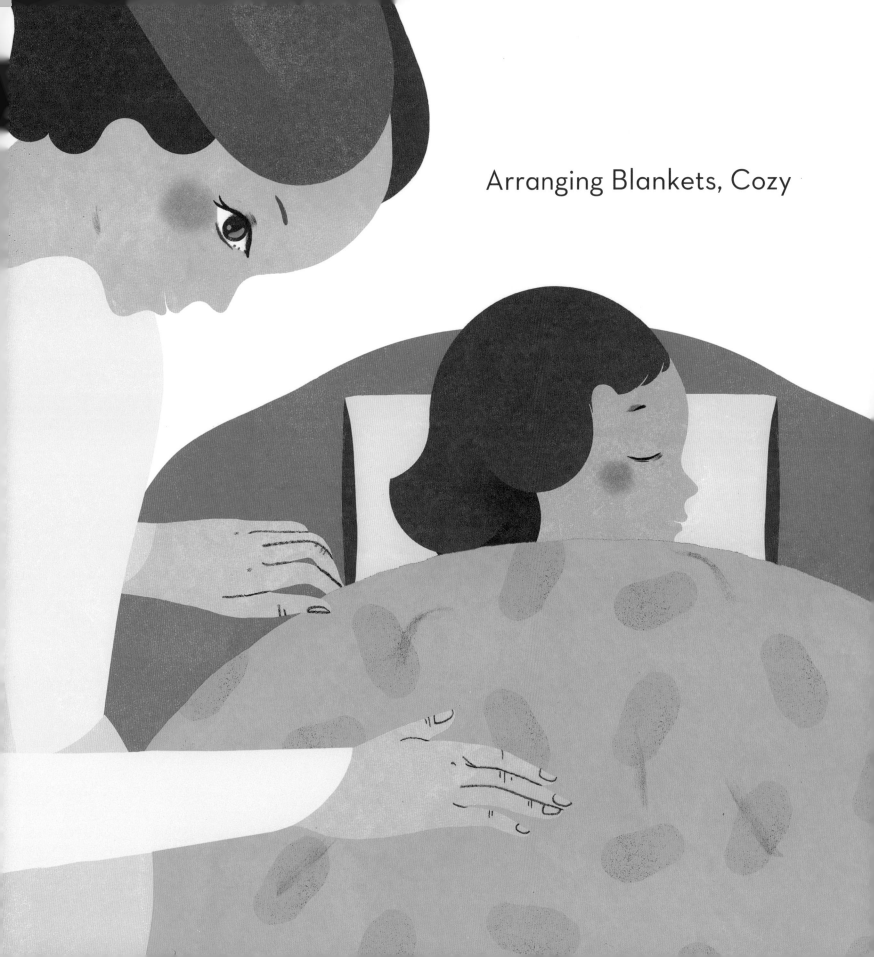

Arranging Blankets, Cozy

Alive. Beloved. Content.

(Alas, Book Concludes)

Afterword (Brief Commentary)

We've sprinkled some ABC words throughout the book. How many can you find?
Here's **A Bitty Clue** to get you started:
what do you see on the boy's bedroom floor that starts with the letter B?

(You'll find a semi-complete list just below—
surely you will spot some words that we missed!)

A: accident, abodes, antennae, aperture, apron, armory, arms, art, asteroid, audience, author

B: ball, bangs, bath, bath towel, bathtub, beak, bear, bed, beret, binoculars, blades (of grass), blocks, blouse, blue, blush, boots, bowling pins, breeze, bristles, brows, brush, buildings

C: cactus, camera, cards, carpet, castle, cattails, chair, chapel, checkers, cheeks, cheers, chick, children, chimneys, choo-choo, church, clapping, click (light off), cliff, cloth, coffee table, coat, collar, comets, constellation, couch, cuff

Amy's Book Contest

We now invite you to create your own ABC phrase and accompanying drawing
(inspired by something in your life or something in this book)
and submit it to:

Amy's Book Contest

849 Valencia Street

San Francisco, CA 94110

We will post as many as we can at mcsweeneys.net/abc

10 children will receive a special prize and an **Awesome Brainy Crown**.

Adios! Bye! Ciao!

Amy (Book's Creator)

Amy Krouse Rosenthal creates books for children (such as this one), books for adults (such as *Encyclopedia of an Ordinary Life*), and tiny films (such as *The Beckoning of Lovely*). She lives on a tree-lined street with her family in Chicago.

Gracia Lam was born in Hong Kong and raised in Toronto. She was a formally trained ballerina before turning to the art of illustration. Her work has been exhibited around the world. *Awake Beautiful Child* is her first book.